CW00841542

LITTLE MISS DAISY

And Her Four Seasons

Anna Oighrig, A Siadar, An Gearasdan, Agus Glaschu

ARTHUR H. STOCKWELL LTD
Torrs Park, Ilfracombe, Devon, EX34 8BA
Established 1898
www.ahstockwell.co.uk

© Anna Oighrig, A Siadar, An Gearasdan, Agus Glaschu, 2020
First published in Great Britain, 2020

The moral rights of the author have been asserted.

All rights reserved.
No part of this publication may be reproduced
or transmitted in any form or by any means,
electronic or mechanical, including photocopy,
recording, or any information storage and
retrieval system, without permission
in writing from the copyright holder.

British Library Cataloguing-in-Publication Data.
A catalogue record for this book is available
from the British Library.

ISBN 978-0-7223-4986-1
Printed in Great Britain by
Arthur H. Stockwell Ltd
Torrs Park   Ilfracombe
Devon EX34 8BA

SPRING

Little Miss Daisy had a lovely cosy bed underneath a large oak tree which sheltered her from the cold snow and frost of winter.

But now she could feel spring in the
air, the sun was a bit warmer and she
could hear the boys and girls out playing.

The tulips and daffodils had woken up
as well, and they all held their heads
up high for all to see just how beautiful
they were.

As the weeks went by, and the days got
warmer and warmer, Little Miss Daisy could
see mums and dads, boys and girls
tenderly hoeing their gardens, and gently forking
the ground so that the flowers could enjoy the
feel of soft loose ground around them.

Little Miss Daisy could hear the
birds singing their spring songs
as they happily built their nests
for the arrival of the baby birds.

Very soon it would be warm enough
for Little Miss Daisy to stay awake
all day and enjoy the hot sun of
summer and the boys and girls would
be out to play.

SUMMER

Little Miss Daisy enjoyed watching
the boys and girls out playing with their
toys; the summer flowers were in
full bloom now too, and how lovely
they looked!

Many of the children had pets to play
with too. Mainly cats, dogs and rabbits.

The weeks went by and the sun grew
hotter and hotter, and the ground became
drier and drier.
'Oh, I would love a drink of water,'
thought Little Miss Daisy. 'I can't be
happy again until I get a drink.'
The rest of the flowers weren't looking
too happy either, and bowed their heads
to the ground.

One morning Little Miss Daisy woke up
to the sound of falling rain.

She shouted to the rest of her flower
friends, "Hey, wake up – it's raining.
We can all have a lovely cool drink of
fresh water."

In fact it rained so much that the children
had to stay indoors in case they got wet.
But the flowers were so happy to get a drink
they lifted their heads up high again.

After a few days the sun came out again.
The flowers were so happy now and Little
Miss Daisy was so pleased for them all.

The children were happy too – they could
get out to play their favourite games
again too.

Summer passes far too quickly though;
soon it would be autumn and the air colder.

AUTUMN

The days were becoming colder now
and the flowers were preparing for
their next big sleep.
In summer their leaves were a lovely
shade of green, but now they had
changed to brown and yellow.

'Oh, it is much colder,' thought Little Miss Daisy.
'Even the boys and girls are wearing extra
clothes to keep them nice and warm.'

Little Miss Daisy inspected her little bed
underneath the large oak tree.

WINTER

Little Miss Daisy lay down to sleep that
night in her cosy little bed.

'It is lovely and warm in here,' she thought,
'but the air is so cold I would not be
surprised if it snows before morning.'

And how right Little Miss Daisy was!
When she woke up in the morning the
ground was white with snow.

The little robins were hopping about
in search of food and the children were
happily playing in the snow.

Little Miss Daisy curled up in her cosy little bed
and whispered, "Goodnight, everybody. See
you again in the spring."